SOPHIE

THE SADDLE

"She's got a nice face," said Sophie.

SOPHIE IN THE SADDLE

DICK KING-SMITH

illustrated by
David Parkins

CANDLEWICK PRESS
CAMBRIDGE, MASSACHUSETTS

First U.S. paperback edition 1999

The Library of Congress has cataloged the hardcover edition as follows:

King-Smith, Dick.
Sophie in the saddle / Dick King-Smith ; illustrated by David Parkins.
—1st U.S. ed.
Summary: Having added the puppy Puddle to her growing menagerie
of cat and rabbit, animal-mad Sophie makes friends with a Vietnamese
pot-bellied pig and a gray pony named Bumblebee.
ISBN 1-56402-329-X (hardcover)
[1. Pets—Fiction.] I. Parkins, David, ill. II. Title.
PZ7.K5893Sm 1994
[E]—dc20 93-26723

ISBN 1-56402-607-8 (paperback)

2 4 6 8 10 9 7 5 3 1

Printed in the United States of America

This book was set in Garamond Book.
The pictures were done in pen and ink.

Candlewick Press
2067 Massachusetts Avenue
Cambridge, Massachusetts 02140

CONTENTS

"Let's call him Puddle," said Sophie.

PUDDLE

Sophie's birthday was on the twenty-fifth of December. Sophie was rather proud of this fact. Ages and ages ago, when she was only four, Sophie had said to her twin brothers Matthew and Mark, "I bet I'm the only girl who was ever born on Christmas Day."

"Course you're not," they said.

"Well, who else was then?" Sophie said. "Go on, tell me."

The twins looked at one another.

"I know!" said Matthew.

"I know what you're going to say!" said Mark.

"Jesus!" they cried.

Sophie looked scornful.

"Funny sort of girl," she said.

She plodded off to ask her mother and father, but they said that thousands of babies were born every day of the year, including Christmas Day.

"So there must be lots of other little girls who share your birthday," her mother said.

"I bet I'm the only one who's going to be a lady farmer," said Sophie.

"Well, that narrows it down a bit," said her father, "but I expect there are quite a number who share your ambition."

"What's an ambition?"

"Something you are determined to do."

Sophie, though small, was very determined, and she was not going to lose this argument.

"I bet," she said, "that I'm the only girl in the world who was born on Christmas Day and is going to be a lady farmer and is going to have a cow called Blossom and two hens called April and May and a pony called Shorty and a pig called Measles."

"Now there," they said, "you may be right."

All that was two years before. Sophie was six now, and the twins were eight — Matthew, as he always would be, ten minutes older than Mark.

Sophie was as determined as ever to be a lady farmer one day. For two years she had been saving up for this. On the side of her piggy bank was stuck a notice. Originally it had said:

Farm munny
thank you
Sophie

*Already Sophie thought of the puppy
as her own.*

But since going to school, Sophie's spelling had improved, and now it read:

Farm monney
thank you
Sophie

At one time there had been ten pounds and ten pence in the piggy bank, but Sophie had spent three pounds of this on a collar and leash for one of her pets. These were a black cat called Tomboy, a white rabbit called Beano, and a puppy, as yet without a name. Strictly speaking, the puppy belonged to all the family, but already Sophie thought of it as her own.

It had arrived this very day, her sixth birthday, the seventh Christmas Day of her life.

In fact Sophie had last used the collar and leash for Beano, so that he could exercise on the lawn, the loop of the leash dropped over a stake around which he grazed in a circle.

"The puppy can have the rabbit's collar and leash now, can't he?" Sophie's mother said that evening.

"No," said Sophie.

"Beano doesn't need them," said Sophie's father. "He's in his nice warm hutch for the winter. And in the summer you can always tether him with a bit of string."

"No," said Sophie.

"Why not?" they said.

"Because I bought them with my farm money. They're mine. And you said the puppy belongs to all of us. So I'll sell you all the collar and leash. You can all pay me for them."

"Not me," said Mark.

"Nor me," said Matthew.

"How much?" said Sophie's father.

Sophie rubbed the tip of her nose, a sure sign that she was thinking deeply.

"To you lot — three pounds, fifty pence," she said.

"How much did you pay for them in the first place?" her mother asked. Sophie did not approve of telling lies.

"Three pounds," she said.

"You're asking more than when they were new!"

"Take it or leave it," said Sophie.

Her father took his pipe out of his mouth to give an admiring whistle.

"Quite the businesswoman," he said. "I can just see you at the market. You'll drive a hard bargain."

"I shan't," said Sophie. "I shall drive a station wagon."

She sat on the floor beside the Christmas

"We're silly, stupid, and sickening!"
chanted the twins.

tree, the new puppy in her lap. He was a little terrier, white except for a black patch over his right eye.

"You haven't got a name, my dear," she said.

"We could call him Pirate," her father said.

"Why?"

"Because he's got a black patch over one eye."

"Or just Patch?" said Sophie's mother.

"Call him Mark," said Matthew.

"Or Matthew," said Mark, and they both giggled.

"You know what you are," said Sophie.

"Yes," they said, for they knew only too well what an angry Sophie always called them. "We're silly, stupid, and sickening!" they chanted, and they rolled around, laughing.

"You're ingerant, you are," said Sophie.

"Ignorant, you mean," they said.

"That too," Sophie said.

She put the puppy down and stood up and

plodded off, shoulders hunched, the picture of disapproval.

"Come on now, Sophie," said her mother. "You choose a name."

"After all, it was you who liked this puppy best," her father said. "Andrew's dad told me."

Sophie's friend Andrew was a farmer's son, and their terrier Lucy was the mother of the nameless puppy.

Sophie turned around.

"Can we call him whatever I choose?" she said.

"If you like."

"Promise?"

"Oh, all right."

At that moment the puppy plodded off into a corner of the room. Here it squatted down and made a little pool on the carpet.

"Look at that!" cried the twins.

Sophie rubbed the tip of her nose

"That's it," she said.

"What's what?" said her parents.

"What he's done. It's given me an idea for a name."

"What?" said everybody.

"Puddle," said Sophie. "Let's call him Puddle."

"Sophie!" said her mother.

"Ugh!" said her brothers.

"Give a dog a bad name," said her father.

"You promised," said Sophie.

So Puddle he was.

Sophie scooped him up and put him out.

JOLLY BRAVE

Apart from that first mistake, Puddle did not live up to his name. By the time Sophie and the boys went back to school after the Christmas holidays, he was pretty well house-broken.

This was largely due to Sophie's efforts. She watched Puddle like a hawk, and the moment he seemed restless or showed any sign of being about to lower himself toward the floor, she scooped him up and put him out in the garden.

All this in turn was thanks to Sophie's aunt Al. Aunt Al was really the children's great-

great-aunt but she was also Sophie's great-great-friend. She was nearly eighty-two years old but extremely young at heart, and she lived in the Highlands, a mysterious-sounding land, Sophie always thought, from which the inhabitants peered down at the rest of the world far below.

It was Aunt Al who had fixed it so that Sophie was allowed to keep a stray black cat, at first called Tom, but later, after giving birth to four kittens, renamed Tomboy.

It was Aunt Al who now owned one of those kittens, called Ollie.

It was Aunt Al who had given Sophie the rabbit, Beano.

And it was Aunt Al who telephoned, a couple of days after Christmas.

Sophie answered the phone.

"It's Aunt Al," she said. "She's calling down

from the Highlands."

"Calling up, you mean," said her father.

Sophie sighed.

"Oh, Daddy," she said. Sophie, in common with her great-great-aunt, liked to speak her mind, but she was wary of telling her father that he was silly, stupid, and sickening. But really! How could you call *up* from the top of the Highlands?

"She wants to speak to you, I expect," said Sophie.

"Who's 'she'? The cat's mother?" said a sharp voice at the other end. "It's you I want to speak to, Sophie."

"Oh."

"You got a nice surprise, didn't you?"

"Oh, yes. Puddle, you mean."

"Is that what the puppy's called?"

"Yes," said Sophie.

"That's what I'm calling you about," said Aunt Al. "I know he's meant to be the family's pet, but your father has his work, and your mother has the house to look after, and the boys won't be the slightest use — always off playing football — so you're going to have to be the dog trainer, Sophie. He's too young to be taught a lot of things yet, but you must get him house-broken. I'll tell you what to do." And she did.

"And if he slips up," said Aunt Al, "don't let anyone shout at him or rub his nose in it — he won't understand. Oh, and by the way, soda water's good for the carpet."

The conversation ended in their usual no-nonsense way.

"Got it?"

"Yes."

"Okay. Ollie sends his love."

"Right."

"Bye."

"Bye."

Sophie put the phone down.

"What was all that about?" asked her mother.

Sophie did not answer directly. Instead she said, "Mom. When was I clean?"

"Clean? Potty-trained, you mean?"

"Yes."

"Oh, about two."

"Two months?"

"Two years!"

"Yikes!" said Sophie.

She picked up the puppy and went out into the garden and put him down on the lawn.

"Now then, my dear," she said, "you haven't even got two weeks before I go back to school, so you'd better get a move on." And when he did, she said, "You *are* clever."

"*Mee-ow?*" said a voice, and Tomboy came to

Puddle received a sharp cuff around the ear.

rub against her legs. Puddle immediately made a bumbling rush at the cat and received a sharp cuff around the ear.

"*Nee-o!*" said Tomboy — or that's what it sounded like — and stalked off.

"Come and see Beano," Sophie said. "He won't hurt you."

Beano lived in a large hutch in the potting shed, where once, when younger, Sophie had kept her flocks and herds of wood lice, worms, centipedes, earwigs, slugs, and snails.

He was a large white rabbit with floppy ears and pink eyes and a wiffly nose. He had never been in the least afraid of Tomboy, and now, when Sophie opened the hutch door and put him down on the floor beside the puppy, he thumped with his hind legs and gave such a threatening growl that Puddle's small tail went between his legs. "Nobody loves you, my dear,"

Sophie said, "except your trainer."

By the end of the school vacation Puddle had learned a lot.

Not to do things—or chew things—in the house.

Not to tangle with cats or rabbits.

To answer to his name.

To walk — after a fashion — on a leash beside Sophie, wearing Beano's old blue collar.

Sophie got up early on the first day of the new term, and dressed—a gray pleated skirt, gray shirt, striped tie, maroon cardigan. At first she had hated her school uniform, but now she was used to it, and by the time she had attended to all her animals no one would have guessed that her clothes had been clean a mere half-hour before. Her dark hair looked, as always, as though she had just come through a hedge backward.

"Looking forward to school, Sophie?" her

father said at breakfast.

"Sort of," Sophie said.

She quite liked school and was interested in some of the things they taught her. It was just a pity there were no farming lessons, nor did they allow you to bring pets.

"You will look after Puddle properly, Mom, won't you?" she said.

"Of course I will."

"He's still only amateur, you see."

"Amateur?"

"Yes, you know, young."

"Oh, you mean immature," her mother said.

"A baby," said Matthew.

"Like Sophie," said Mark.

"And all her little friends," said Matthew.

"Like Duncan," said Mark.

Duncan was a small, fat boy whom Sophie had once considered employing as a farm worker at some time in the future.

"He's stupid," said Sophie.

"And Dawn," said Matthew.

"Yuck!" said Sophie.

Dawn was a pretty little girl with golden hair done in pigtails. Sophie had often been tempted to give them a good tug. They did not get along.

"And Andrew," said Mark.

"Sophie likes Andrew," they giggled.

Sophie's face darkened, but before she could utter her usual comment her father said, "Wonder if they've sold the other five pups?"

Sophie forgot about her brothers' teasing and looked thoughtful.

"Suppose there was just one left," she said. "All alone."

"No, Sophie," said her father firmly. "We are not having any more animals in this house."

That evening Sophie lay in the bathtub, playing with a very lifelike rubber frog.

Puddle sat on the bath mat, whining. Perhaps on account of his name, he seemed to love water. He liked to jump in any pools left lying after the rain, and he longed to join Sophie in the bathtub.

School had been much as Sophie had expected. Dawn was just as yucky, Duncan was just as stupid, Andrew was just as nice, and they still didn't give farming lessons.

Lucy's other puppies had all been sold, Andrew told her, but he had asked her and Puddle to lunch next Saturday, which was nice. Or rather Sophie had told Andrew to ask his mother to ask them, which she did.

Sophie squeezed the rubber frog's stomach and it let out a loud squeak, much to Puddle's

"Wish I could swim," said Sophie.

excitement. Her mother came into the bath-
room in time to hear Sophie say, "This is a frog
and he's amphigorous."

"He's amphibious," her mother said.

"That's what I said," replied Sophie, launch-
ing the frog back into the water.

"Wish I could swim," she said.

"Can you swim?" she said to Andrew next
Saturday, as they went on a tour of the farm-
yard, Andrew leading, Sophie plodding behind,
Puddle following.

"Yes, course I can," said Andrew, his stock
answer. If Sophie had asked whether he
could fly, the reply would probably have been
the same.

"I'm a brilliant swimmer, I am," he said.

"Matthew and Mark can swim like fishes,"
Sophie said, "but I can't."

Just then they came upon the duck pond. It was a large duck pond, and around its rim a number of ducks were standing and preening their feathers. At the sight of them Puddle ran forward, yapping with excitement, and the ducks, quacking with dismay, took to the water. Puddle leapt in after them.

"He'll be drowned!" shouted Sophie, and she jumped in after Puddle.

Andrew's father, attracted by all the noise, arrived in time to see a remarkable scene.

On the bank Andrew was rolling around, laughing fit to burst.

In the pond the puppy was swimming around and around with an expert doggy paddle in pursuit of the ducks.

Sophie was standing waist-deep in the filthy water. "Yuck!" she cried. "I'm stuck in the duck muck!"

"He'll be drowned!" shouted Sophie.

* * *

"Andrew's dad pulled me out," Sophie said later, at home.

"And didn't you stink!" said Mark.

"You still do," said Matthew.

"The first time you went to that farm," Sophie's mother said, "you fell in a cowpat."

"Why in the world did you jump into the duck pond?" her father said.

"I thought Puddle would drown," Sophie said. "I didn't know he could swim."

"But you can't. And it might have been deep."

"I didn't think of that," Sophie said.

Matthew and Mark looked at their small but determined sister. Then they looked at one another.

Then, with one voice, they said, "You were jolly brave."

Sophie grinned.

"Was I?" she said.

"One thing's certain," said her father. "It's high time you learned to swim."

"And before the end of the spring too," her mother said.

"Why?" said Sophie.

"Because we're all going on vacation to the seaside this year."

"Yikes!" cried Sophie. "All of us?"

"Yes."

"Tomboy?"

"No."

"Beano?"

"No."

Sophie put on her most determined face.

"If Puddle can't go," she said, "I'm not coming."

"If you learn to swim properly," her father said, "then Puddle can come."

"I'll learn," said Sophie.

"Yikes!" said Sophie. "Whatever sort is that?"

A Nasty Shock

Sophie was as good as her word.

In the spring term the school children went, once a week, to the local swimming pool, and by May Sophie had swum a width. She was not a graceful swimmer like Matthew and Mark, who could do a flashy crawl. Both twins were fast runners, winning all their races in school sports, and swimming for them was just another form of racing.

Sophie, by contrast, sploshed along, using a stroke much like Puddle's, but she kept doggedly on, blowing like a whale, determined not to give up. Just before the end of the term, she swam a length of the pool.

She came out of school with a big grin on her face.

"You look pleased with yourself," her mother said. "What have you been up to?"

"I done it!" said Sophie.

"Done what — I mean, did what?"

"Swum a length of the pool. I can swim properly. So Puddle can come with us to the seaside, can't he?"

The twins came racing up, dead-heating as usual.

"Mom!" they shouted in unison. "Sophie's swum a length!"

"She wasn't very fast," said Matthew. "She took ages."

"But she kept going," said Mark, "and she never put her feet down on the bottom once."

"Course not," said Sophie. She did not approve of cheating.

The whole conversation was repeated that evening, when the children's father returned from work.

"Well done, Sophie," he said, and he looked at his wife.

"We can tell them now, can't we?" he said, and she nodded.

"Tell us what?" they all said.

"Well, you see, the idea of taking Puddle with us complicated things a bit. Hotels and boarding houses don't allow dogs. So we're going to stay somewhere where they do. It's only about three miles from the sea, so we can get to the beach in no time."

"And I think you'll all like it," said the children's mother.

"Especially Sophie."

"Why 'specially me?" said Sophie.

"Because we're going to stay on a farm."

Sophie's cry of "*Yikes!*" was the loudest they had ever heard. When her parents came to say good night to her that evening, she was lying in bed looking at pictures on her bedroom wall — the four pictures, drawn by her mother, of Blossom, of April and May, of Shorty, and of Measles.

"Will they have spotty pigs on this farm?" she said.

"Don't know. Perhaps. It says they have all sorts of different animals."

"Cows?"

"Probably."

"And hens?"

"Sure to."

"And Shetland ponies?"

"Don't know about Shetlands. They've got ponies. For riding."

"Yikes!" said Sophie very softly. "I could ride."

"You'll have to learn how to properly," they said.

"I'll learn," said Sophie.

The final days of the spring term dragged by, but at last came the magic moment when the car was loaded and the whole family, including Puddle, was ready to set off for Cornwall and the sea.

"Don't forget my boots," Sophie had said when they were packing.

"Boots? On the beach?"

"On the farm," Sophie said.

Tomboy and Beano were to be looked after by a kind neighbor during the two weeks' holiday. Sophie had given strict instructions about their welfare.

"There's plenty of hay and rabbit mixture for Beano," she said, "and what sort of bread do you have?"

"Whole wheat," said the neighbor. "Why?"

"He likes that," Sophie said. "The crusts. If you could spare some now and then? Lightly toasted."

Tomboy was to have the run of the kitchen via the cat flap. "But," said Sophie, "she is to have water to drink, not milk, it makes her fat. But she can have as much canned cat food as she wants."

"Won't that make her fat?" said the neighbor.

"No," said Sophie. "It's full of protons and carbonhydrons, all different flavors—her favorite's tuna."

* * *

42

Now Sophie sat between the boys on the back seat, Puddle on her lap. He was nine months old now and as well trained as small terriers ever can be, which isn't very well, as a rule.

He would walk on a leash without pulling, and come when called, and sit when told, but the command "Stay!" didn't mean much to him since he liked always to be on the go.

"He'll love the sea, won't he?" said Sophie.

"We all shall, I hope," said her mother. "Especially if this fine weather keeps up. Let's just hope it doesn't rain."

"Farmers need rain," said Sophie.

"Not while we're on holiday they don't," said her father.

"Or only at night," said her mother.

It was a long drive, and it was almost dark by the time they arrived, too late to think of going to the beach that day. But the farmer and his wife were very welcoming and they had a daughter of about Sophie's age called Jo.

When she was introduced, Sophie eyed Jo with some suspicion for she was quite a pretty girl, not unlike the dreaded Dawn, to look at. However, she wore her fair hair short, and she had a friendly smile. More, she was wearing boots and old scruffy clothes and she smelled quite strongly of pig, so Sophie was reassured.

Next morning, Sophie woke up early and looked out of the window of the funny little attic room that was to be hers and Puddle's for the two weeks.

She could see cows coming in for milking, and sheep in a field, and ponies in a paddock, and hens and ducks and geese in the yard, and she knew there must be at least one pig

*Jo was wearing boots and old scruffy clothes
and she smelled quite strongly of pig.*

because of the smell of the farmer's daughter.

So she got dressed and tiptoed downstairs, Puddle following, and put on her boots and went out. Jo, she found, was up already, crossing the yard with a bucket in her hand and a couple of collies at her heels, and she said "Hello," and the farm dogs sniffed at Puddle and wagged their tails.

"Hello," Sophie said. "Do you have pigs?"

"One," said Jo. "Just one."

"Is it a spotty one?"

"A Gloucester Old Spots, d'you mean?"

"Yes," said Sophie. "I've seen them. At the Royal Wessex Agricultural Show. I'm going to be a lady farmer, you see. Is your pig one of those?"

"No," said Jo. "I'm just going to feed him. You can come too if you like."

So Sophie plodded after her till they came to an old-fashioned brick-built pigsty, and there was the oddest-looking pig she had ever seen.

It was a dirty blackish color, and very fat, with very short legs and a short wrinkled neck and a huge stomach that almost brushed the ground.

"Yikes!" said Sophie. "Whatever sort is that?"

"He's a Vietnamese potbellied pig," said Jo. "He's my special pet. My dad thought up a special name for him."

"What?" said Sophie.

"Big-fat-tum," said Jo.

Sophie, now also smelling of pig, ate an enormous breakfast, and then the family piled into the car and set off for the sea.

The beach was wide and sandy, with rocks to climb and pools to paddle in, and the sea was calm, and there weren't too many people around, and the sun shone in a cloudless sky.

They all swam, including Puddle of course, and it was easier in the sea, Sophie found. Matthew and Mark went off with a football and in no time at all they had found some other boys and started a game. And Sophie's mom and dad lay in the sun.

Sophie made a sandcastle, except that it was really a sandfarmhouse, with a sandcowshed and a sandpigsty, and altogether everything was lovely.

"Happy, Sophie?" they said, and Sophie nodded.

I am, she thought. I like being on the beach and swimming, and I like my little bedroom, and Jo, she's all right, and Big-fat-tum, he's amazing, and I don't see what could spoil this holiday.

She got up from her building and called Puddle.

"I'm going for a walk along the beach," she

said, "to get some shells."

"Not too far," they said. "Not out of our sight."

"Okay," Sophie said.

She had not gone far when she came to a biggish rock that stuck up in the beach. Some people were sitting on the far side of this rock, a mother and father and a girl, and as Sophie approached, the girl got up and ran down toward the water.

She was a long-legged girl in a bright pink swimsuit and her golden hair was done in pigtails, tied with green ribbon.

It was Dawn.

Sophie plodded back with a face like thunder.

BUMBLEBEE

Sophie plodded back with a face like thunder. She arrived at the same time as the twins, who came racing up and threw themselves across an imaginary finish line, completely destroying Sophie's sandfarm. Sophie didn't even notice.

"Guess who I've just seen," she said in tones of deepest gloom.

"Haven't a clue," said her father.

"Someone from school," said Sophie.

"Someone you don't much like, by the look of you," said her mother.

"I know!" said Mark.

"I know what you're going to say!" said Matthew.

"Dawn!" they shouted.

"Oh, no!" said her parents.

"Oh, yes," said Sophie. "She's just down the beach, with her horrible mom and her horrible dad."

"How d'you know they're horrible?"

"Well, they had Dawn, didn't they?"

"I think you should try to be nicer to poor Dawn," said Sophie's mother. "She can't be all that bad."

"Yuck!" said Sophie.

Long long ago Dawn had deliberately squashed one of the largest of Sophie's herd of wood lice, and Sophie had neither forgotten nor forgiven.

The twins looked slyly at one another and grinned.

"Now you've got someone to play with," they said with one voice. Sophie turned an angry face upon them, and then saw the wreck of her sandfarm.

"Look what you've done!" she shouted. "You're silly, stupid, and sickening, you are!" and she charged furiously at them, but they ran away laughing.

"Calm down, Sophie," said her father. "I'll help you build another one."

"I don't want to build another one."

"Well, let's go and have another swim."

"I don't want another swim."

"Or throw sticks into the sea for Puddle."

"Don't want to."

"Well, what do you want then?"

"I want to go back to the farm."

"Not yet," said her father. "This weather's too good to miss. We shan't be going for hours yet."

"Cheer up, Sophie darling," said her mother. "Let's have our picnic lunch."

"Not hungry," said Sophie.

But in fact she found she was, and she was still eating when everyone else was full. And afterward, Matthew and Mark helped her to build a simply enormous sandcastle and dug tunnels through it and decorated it with seaweed and shells and pebbles, and finally wrote in the sand with a piece of driftwood:

Sophie's Castle Keep Out

"And put 'Trespassers will be persecuted,'" said Sophie.

"Prosecuted," said her father.

"Yes, and prosecuted too," said Sophie. "Like that Dawn ought to be, for coming on our beach."

This gave her an idea, and she took the piece of driftwood and went along to the big sticking-up rock, cautiously, in case they were still there. But they weren't, so Sophie wrote in the sand in huge letters:

Go hom Dawn

That'll scare her, she thought. She never saw me so it'll be really spooky for her to see her name there tomorrow; and at the end of the day Sophie went home much happier, while the incoming tide crept up the beach and washed out her message.

By bedtime Sophie had quite recovered her spirits. She had been allowed to feed Big-fattum, she had helped pick up the eggs in the henhouse, she had spoken to some sheep and chatted to some cows, and finally Jo had taken her around the stables and showed her some of the ponies, for the next day Sophie was to have her first riding lesson.

"I expect my mom will put you up on this one," Jo said, stroking the velvety muzzle of a gray pony that was looking out over the half-door of its box. "She's called Bumblebee. She's a beginner's pony."

"She's got a nice face," said Sophie.

"She's as quiet as an old sheep," said Jo.

"She's as quiet as an old sheep," said Jo's mother the next morning as she saddled up Bumblebee.

Sophie's father and the twins had gone to the beach, while her mother stayed behind to watch the first lesson.

"Only one thing Bumblebee doesn't like," said the farmer's wife, "and that's pigs. Which is one reason why we don't keep any, apart from that ugly old creature of Jo's."

"Why doesn't she like pigs?" asked Sophie.

A person who didn't like pigs would be foolish, she thought, so perhaps this was a foolish horse.

"Some horses are funny about things," the farmer's wife said. "We had a pony that was frightened stiff of the local bus—go mad, he would, if the bus came along. And another that hated going through gateways. Bumblebee, she can't stand pigs. Now then, Sophie, ever been on a horse before?"

"No," said Sophie, "but I'm going to be a lady farmer, so I shall have to know how to ride a horse around my flocks and herds."

"A lady farmer, eh? Not going to have a man around the place, then?"

"I might," said Sophie. "I might marry Andrew, but only if he's got a farm. If he hasn't, I shan't."

"Very sensible," said the farmer's wife. "Now then, let's get you up. You're not nervous, are you?"

"No," said Sophie. She was, a tiny bit, but she wasn't going to say so. All the same it felt very odd once she was sitting on Bumblebee's back. The pony was not a big one, but it did seem to Sophie that she was rather a long way from the ground.

Jo's mother showed her how to hold the reins, and how her feet should be in the irons ("toes to Heaven, heels to Hell"), and told her to sit up straight and to keep her hands low. Then she said, "Now, all we're going to do is to walk along nice and quiet, with me holding the leading rein. Ready?"

"Just a minute," said Sophie's mother, and she took out her camera so she could take a picture of stocky Sophie sitting on stocky Bumblebee.

"Cheese, Sophie!" she cried, but Sophie's face was grimly determined under the hard hat.

"That cap I gave her looks a bit small," the farmer's wife said. "Jo's would fit her better, I think," and she called, "Jo!"

"Yes?" came a voice from the far side of the yard.

"Can you come here a minute, please? Quickly."

Jo was in the pigsty, scratching the bristly back of her Vietnamese potbellied pet, who had lowered himself a few inches to lie blissfully on his fat stomach.

"Stay there, Big-fat-tum," she said. "Back in a second," and she ran out of the sty. She pulled the door closed but did not bother to latch it. Slowly, it swung open again.

The procession had only just started out — the farmer's wife, leading Bumblebee, Sophie, now wearing Jo's hat, sitting as straight as a ramrod, her mother walking behind — when around the corner came the small, fat, bristly black shape of Big-fat-tum, squealing happily to himself at this unexpected freedom.

Bumblebee let out a shrill neigh of horror and shied violently, and Sophie came off with a thump.

Her mother rushed to her.

"It's all right, darling," she said. "Don't cry."

"I'm not," said Sophie.

Sophie did not approve of crying.

"Get that pig of yours out of here, Jo!" shouted the farmer's wife angrily, and to Sophie she said, "Have you hurt yourself?"

Sophie came off with a thump.

"No," said Sophie. She had, a tiny bit, but she wasn't going to say so.

"Perhaps we'd better leave it at that for today," her mother said.

"No," said Sophie. "I want to try again."

"She's quite right," said the farmer's wife. She lowered her voice. "Best thing to do, get straight on again," she murmured. "Otherwise she might lose her nerve."

Sophie's mother smiled.

"Not Sophie," she said.

"Come on, then," said the farmer's wife. "Up we go."

"Can I say something to Bumblebee first?" Sophie asked.

"Of course, if you want to."

Sophie plodded around and reached up to the gray pony's head and stroked her nose.

"Now then, my dear," she said. "You listen to

me. The P-I-G has gone, so there's no need to be frightened anymore."

"I thought I'd better spell it," she said, once she was astride again. "You never know how much animals can understand."

"No doubt about it," said the farmer's wife to Sophie's mother. "She's going to be a proper lady farmer, she is. Walk on!"

"Jo's mom said I had a good seat," said Sophie.

The Rescue

Sophie's words seemed to have calmed Bumblebee, who was as quiet and sheeplike as you could wish for the rest of the ride.

Afterward Sophie's mother found her standing with her back to a long looking-glass, peering around at her reflection.

"Whatever are you doing?" she asked.

"Jo's mom said I had a good seat," said Sophie, "so I was just looking at it."

Her mother laughed.

"She meant you sat naturally on a horse," she said, "and so you did. Some people ride like sacks of potatoes, but I think you're going to be a good horsewoman."

"Horsegirl," said Sophie.

"How did you get on?" her father said when he came back.

"I got off," said Sophie.

"She fell off," said her mother, "but she got straight on again."

"That's my girl," said Sophie's father. "Small you may be, but determined you certainly are."

After that the holiday developed a pattern. Sophie had her riding lessons first thing after breakfast, and then they all spent the day together on the beach.

At first Sophie had tried to persuade them to go to a different, Dawn-free beach, but they said no, this was the nicest and the nearest and anyway with a bit of luck Dawn and her parents might go somewhere else.

Which they must have done, because

although Sophie went off scouting each morning along the sands — in disguise, that is to say wearing her mother's dark glasses and with a sun hat pulled well down — there was no sign of them.

"She must have read my notice," said Sophie to Puddle.

Puddle was blissfully happy. Everything about the holiday suited him down to the ground. At night he slept in Sophie's room, supposedly in his basket but actually on her bed. Then there was the farm, with all its exciting sounds and smells, and his friends, the two collies. And lastly there was the sea, that lovely great watery paradise into which he plunged on any excuse and in which he swam tirelessly around, looking, with that black patch over one eye, the perfect pirate dog.

In general, he behaved very well, but he did

have one bad habit. He would stand in front of anyone on the beach who was playing with a ball or a Frisbee, and yap at them.

What he was saying was as plain as could be.

"My family isn't throwing sticks for me just at the moment, so why don't you throw that ball or that Frisbee, and I'll bring it back to you and we can have a lovely game?"

Very occasionally some stranger would take notice of this request, but mostly people told him to buzz off, or else someone in Sophie's family would call him back to them.

But one morning in the second week of the holiday Puddle had wandered a little farther than usual along the beach, when he came upon a girl in a bright pink swimsuit, with golden hair done in pigtails, tied with green ribbon.

Dawn was sitting on the sand, midway

between the big sticking-up rock where her parents were, and the sea. She was playing with a Barbie doll that was almost a miniature of herself, pigtails and all, and Puddle rushed up to her with a volley of barks that said, "Chuck it for me! Go on, chuck it, and I'll bring it back, or I might chew it a bit, it looks good enough to chew. Go on, chuck it!"

Dawn was terrified. She was scared of dogs anyway, and now suddenly out of nowhere had come this strange, noisy, piratical terrier, whose mouth, every yap showed, was full of sharp white teeth. She leapt to her feet and fled.

For Puddle this all added to the fun, and he gave chase, bouncing like a rubber ball beside her and snapping at the Barbie doll, till Dawn, bleating "Mommy! Daddy! Help!" tripped and fell.

At this point Sophie appeared, plodding

Puddle tried madly to grab the doll in his jaws.

along in search of Puddle, only to see him apparently attacking a fallen child.

Then everything happened at once.

Puddle, trying madly to grab the doll in his jaws, suddenly received a hefty slap from Sophie and heard a furious shout of "Stop that, you bad dog, and get away!" and ran off.

Dawn's mother and father, rushing to the rescue, saw only that their precious daughter had been saved from a savage dog attack by a stocky, dark-haired and apparently fearless little girl.

And Dawn, once she had stopped howling, saw Sophie. Sophie's face was a picture.

Fancy going to the help of that wimp Dawn! If only she'd realized in time she wouldn't have slapped poor Puddle, she'd have encouraged him. All he was trying to do was to chew up that revolting Barbie doll.

She turned to go back and make it up with the now distant Puddle, when Dawn's father said, "That was very brave of you, young lady."

"Brave?" said Sophie.

"Yes, rescuing my little girl from that vicious dog."

"He's not . . .," began Sophie, at the same time as Dawn said to her mother, "It's Sophie. From school."

"Sophie?" said Dawn's mother in horrified tones, remembering their first meeting when, after the squashing of the wood louse, Sophie had taken Dawn's toy pony Twinkletoes and solemnly jumped up and down on it until it was a dirty squashed lump.

"From the same school, are you?" said Dawn's father. "Well, well! It's a small world! Fancy you two friends meeting so far from home!"

"She's not . . .," began Dawn and Sophie

at the same time, but Dawn's father, who obviously liked the sound of his own voice, continued.

"Now then, young lady, we're very grateful to you for what you did. Our Dawn might have been badly bitten by that nasty vicious brute, and so might you."

"But . . .," said Sophie.

"No buts," said Dawn's father, and he put his hand in the pocket of his shorts and took out two one-pound coins and held them out to Sophie.

"Here," he said, "I should like you to accept these — they'll buy you a few ice creams — and once again, many thanks for what you did."

"Yes, thank you," said Dawn's mother, rather unwillingly. "Dawn, what do you say to Sophie?"

"Thank you," said Dawn, very unwillingly.

Sophie took the coins. She opened her

mouth and then shut it again. Then she said "Thanks" and plodded off.

Afterward everyone started laughing when she told them what had happened.

"Dawn's father gave you two pounds?" cried Matthew.

"For rescuing her from Puddle?" cried Mark.

"But surely he wasn't trying to bite her?" said Sophie's mother

"No, he was trying to get her beastly Barbie doll."

"Tell us again," said her father, "what they called him."

"A nasty vicious brute," said Sophie.

She cuddled Puddle.

"You are a very good boy," she said, "and I'm sorry I slapped you."

"Talk about getting money under false pretenses!" said her father. "You really should have told them he was your dog."

"He isn't. He's ours."

"Well, ours then."

"I tried," said Sophie, "but they wouldn't listen. So I thought, well, that's another two pounds for my Farm Money. Every little bit helps."

"As the old lady said," added Matthew.

"When she peed in the sea," ended Mark.

"Next summer," smiled the fisherman,
"you'll be growed up like a runner bean."

A Red-Letter Day

The next day was wet, so they drove to the nearest large town. They went into a big department store, partly to get out of the rain, partly — even if they didn't buy anything — to have something to eat and drink in its café, and partly because the children liked riding up and down on the escalators.

Not surprisingly, Sophie's method of travel was not the same as the twins'. They ran up the Up escalators and down the Down, racing one another as always, while Sophie stood stock-still, feet together, on one step, enjoying the sensation of being lifted or dropped without any effort on her part.

At one point, Matthew and Mark stood at the bottom of a Down escalator, looking up as the steps fell toward them.

"I know!" said Mark.

"I know what you're going to say!" said Matthew.

"And so do I," said their father, "and the answer is most certainly No. You two are not going to try to run up the Down one, nor down the Up one for that matter. It's not allowed and it would be very dangerous, so forget it."

There were notices everywhere in the store, telling people where different things were sold. One, Sophie saw, said:

MENSWEAR

She did not comment on this, but a little later

they came upon:

CHILDRENSWEAR

Sophie pointed at it.

"They shouldn't," she said.

"Who shouldn't?"

"Children shouldn't."

"Shouldn't what?"

"Swear," said Sophie.

They all laughed at that.

"Oh, Sophie!" her mother said. "You are a hoot!"

Sophie was not sure what a hoot was, and she did not like being laughed at in what she thought was a silly, stupid, and sickening way. So she hunched her shoulders and stumped along behind, scowling. But two jelly dough-nuts and a large chocolate ice cream in the café cheered her up a bit.

"Only three more days left," her father said, stirring his coffee.

"And we still haven't sent a single postcard to any of our family or friends," said her mother. "It's always the same — we never remember until we're almost home again."

So then they went to the stationery department and chose their own cards.

Sophie was looking for two — one to send to Aunt Al up on top of the Highlands, and one to send to Tomboy and Beano at home.

Aunt Al's was easy — Sophie found a picture of a big black cat that she was sure must be the spitting image of Ollie — but it was more difficult to find a card that would suit both her own cat *and* Beano. At last she did. It was a picture of a fieldmouse (which Tomboy would like) sitting amongst some nice green grass (which Beano would like).

Back at the farm, she wrote them.

On the one for Tomboy and Beano she just put:

Love from Sophie

"No use putting a lot of stuff on it," she said. "After all, they can't read."

With Aunt Al's she took more trouble:

We are staying on a farm
and I am having riding lessons
and I love them and tomorow
I am going to lern to jump.
lots of love to you and Ollie
from Sophie

Sophie's riding lessons had gone very well.

Free from the menace of Big-fat-tum, Bumble-bee had behaved perfectly, and soon there had been no further need of the leading rein. Sophie had learned to stop and start and steer the gray pony, and to rise to the trot, and had even managed a gentle controlled canter.

But she wanted more. She saw Jo (an experienced horsegirl) take her own pony, Nipper, over the course of jumps set out around the paddock, and Jo made it look so easy.

"Can I try a jump?" she asked Jo's mother.

"It's early days for that, I think, Sophie," Jo's mother said. "Perhaps next year, if you come again, which I hope you will."

Sophie looked so downcast that Jo's mother said, "Perhaps tomorrow we'll let you have a try at a very little jump."

That tomorrow had been the rainy day, but at the end of it Sophie went to bed thinking that next morning she would not just ride around, but actually leap over an obstacle.

"Like a swallow," she said to Puddle, "because I have a natural seat and when I grow up I'm going to be a very good horsewoman and I shall probably win lots of horse shows."

If Puddle could have understood and answered this, he would probably have said "Oh, yeah? And I'll be a prizewinning poodle," but as it was, he just jumped up on the bed and they went to sleep.

Sophie's father usually settled down with his pipe and a newspaper during the hour's riding lesson after breakfast, while the twins kicked a football around on the farmhouse lawn, but on this day Sophie wasn't having that.

"You've all got to come and watch this morning," she said. "I'm going to jump Bumblebee."

"Jump over her, d'you mean?" said Matthew.

Not only did Sophie look good,
she performed perfectly.

"Jump on top of her like you jumped on Dawn's Twinkletoes?" said Mark.

"Don't tease, boys," said their mother. "You'll be surprised how well Sophie's riding has come along."

They were, too. They all came—Jo and her father as well—and watched as Jo's mother put Sophie and Bumblebee through their paces.

"Isn't it odd?" said Sophie's father to his wife. "No one could say that Sophie was exactly graceful on the ground, or athletic like the boys. She's more of a plodder. Yet she looks really good on that pony."

Not only did Sophie look good, she performed perfectly.

To be sure, the first jump she was asked to tackle was just a pole laid on the ground, which Bumblebee hopped over, but Sophie looked as proud as if it had been a five-barred gate.

And then Jo's mom put the pole up on some bricks so that it was a foot off the ground, and they jumped it beautifully, and everybody clapped.

"You were really good, Sophie," said her father afterward.

"Not as good as Jo is."

"Well, she's been at it much longer."

"She's lucky, Jo is," Sophie said.

"Living on a farm, you mean?"

"Yes. But 'specially having a pony of her own. Daddy, d'you think . . . ?"

"No, Sophie love," said her father. "You have a cat and a rabbit and one-fifth of a dog, but you are *not* having a pony."

"Okay," said Sophie. "I just thought I'd ask."

* * *

The last morning of the seaside holiday came and a beautiful one it was. They had had good weather all along except for the one wet day, but this one was perfect — hot, but not too hot, and cloudless, with a nice breeze off a sunlit sea.

Sophie had her final riding lesson, and jumped Bumblebee over a pole that was a good two feet off the ground. Then they drove down to the beach, and swam and played, and had a lovely picnic, and never saw hide nor hair of Dawn.

And to cap it all, in the afternoon, Sophie's father hired a boat, and a nice old Cornish fisherman took them out into the bay, and Puddle jumped overboard and had to be rescued. They put out some lines for mackerel but didn't catch anything, which Sophie was glad about, because she thought it must be very painful to have a little hook in your mouth.

And afterward, when the old fisherman put them ashore, he shook hands with everyone in turn.

When he came to Sophie he said, "And how old be you, m'dear?"

"Six," said Sophie.

The old fisherman smiled down at her.

"Next summer," he said, "when you do come back to Cornwall, you'll be growed up like a runner bean."

Afterward Sophie said, "Shall we come back next summer?"

"Let's!" said the twins.

"We might," said their mother.

"We'll see," said their father.

The next morning, while the car was being packed up, Sophie went around with Jo to say good-bye—to the cows and the sheep and the hens and the ducks and the geese, and to Big-fat-tum, and to Nipper and the other horses and ponies, and, last of all, to Bumblebee.

"Good-bye, my dear," she said to the gray pony. "Be good, and keep away from that P-I-G, and I'll see you in a year."

"It's an awful long time to wait," she said to Jo.

"Isn't there a riding school near where you live?" Jo said.

"I expect so," said Sophie.

"Well, you ought to go on with your lessons. You're going to be good—Mom says so. Then next year you'd be able to ride really well and go over all these jumps—you could ride my Nipper if you like."

"Gosh, thanks," said Sophie. "But I've only got twelve pounds and sixty pence Farm Money, and riding lessons are sure to be expensive."

"Ask your mom and dad."

"They'll say 'Wait till next summer.'"

"Riding lessons are expensive," they said when Sophie asked them. "Wait till next summer."

Sophie felt sad as they drove away, sad at leaving Jo and her mom and dad and all the animals, sad at leaving the sea in which she and Puddle had doggy-paddled around so happily.

Then she went to sleep.

When she woke up again they were almost home, and then very soon she was stroking Tomboy and petting Beano, and unpacking in her own room with the pictures of Blossom and April and May and Shorty and Measles.

"Sophie!" her mother called from downstairs. "There's a letter for you."

Sophie plodded downstairs, frowning in thought.

Who could it be from?

She looked at the handwriting on the envelope. It seemed familiar.

She looked at the postmark. DRUMOCHTER, it said.

She opened the envelope.

Dear Sophie,

    Thanks for your postcard. Glad you are having a nice time. I am well and so is Ollie. Interested to hear you are learning to ride. I was pretty good on a horse seventy years ago.

                  Love from Aunt Al

PS Why not get your mother and father to find out if there's a good riding school near you where

you could have a course of lessons? It would make
a nice combined Christmas and seventh birthday
present, wouldn't it?

PTO

They wouldn't pay for a course of lessons, Sophie thought. It's too expensive — they said so.

"What does PTO mean?" she said.

"Please Turn Over."

Sophie turned over the page of writing paper, and read:

PPS A present from me, I meant.

A. A.

And from Sophie there came a great cry of "Yikes!"

THE

END